[UNTITLED]

BY

DERICK D. WRIGHT

(Phone ringing) "Hey mom! How you are doing?" I said.

"I'm great son. Where are you?" She replied.

"Ma, I can't tell you that. As a matter of fact, I can't talk now." I replied.

"But I miss…"

I hung up the phone before she could finish her sentence. I often think about the toll this life has taken on the people who are close to me. as I sit here daydreaming, I think about how life used to be. So simple, but I feel like this was my calling. Now I wonder how far this journey will take me.

"Open the door now! We know you're in here!"

Though I sit here in a daze, I hear this loud screaming from outside my door. I guess this could be the end of the journey perhaps.

Boom! Down comes my front door as police enter my home. I'm already on the floor with my hands behind my head. I knew, if given a reason, the police would have definitely taken me out. Especially considering the things I've been accused of.

Mr. Farran, you're under arrest!

I chuckled as they said my name. I go by Raheem Farran, its just an alias. I felt the need to not go by my government name after a while. My previous charges included; racketeering, conspiracy, murder, capital murder, kidnapping, domestic terrorism, etc. Charges that I beat. So, what the hell am I under arrest for?

"You know you one dumb nigger." Said one of the officers.

"Excuse me, watch your fucking tone and please refrain from speaking with me until we reach the station." I replied fiercely.

I see them look at each other and laugh. I overheard one of them say, "station?" as I sat there, I began to get a bit nervous. I haven't felt fearful in so long. The longer we ride, the more I think back on things wondering was it all worth it. Was I wrong? I feel the car gradually slowing down as we approach literally nothing. I began to do the math, white police, black man/criminal. I may just die here...

"Alright, get out boy!" The officers said to me.

"No sir." I replied calmly

They proceeded to drag me from the vehicle. All I see around me is wooded area and two police. I close my eyes as I began to talk to The Creator. Before I could get my words out a gunshot rang out. Pow! I was shot. I looked down and noticed a hole in my side the size of a bowl. I collapsed immediately. There I lay bleeding as the police sped off. Was this it for me? I close my eyes as fatigue begins to set in. Now, nothing, just darkness...

Well, lets talk about how I got here shall we? I was just a regular guy. I worked as a manager in a grocery store. I have a wife and two kids. I was known as a people person by my peers. Everyone, from customers to coworkers, spoke highly of me. Being very outspoken and confident led to my positive impact on the people who knew me. in my eyes my life was perfect, quote on quote. Why in the hell would I change that? I feel like I worked so hard to get here. Oh, and perfect might not be the correct description, but things could be much worse so no complaints here.

"Excuse me sir, do you work here?" Said a customer in the store.

"Yes ma'am, I do." I replied

"I need help reaching something. You mind helping me?" she asked

"Yes, I'll be right there." I replied respectfully

I realize I had never seen her in the store before. She was a young white lady. I'd say maybe early 20s. as I make my way to her, I noticed her eye contact instantly. She then smiled and looked away. In my head I'm thinking, nope not this time. Infidelity was a problem I had to work out before in my marriage. I swore to myself, this time I would not slip up. I retrieved the item for her. As she took it from me, she smiled and asked, "what's your name?" I looked down at my nametag and she laughed. "oh, I'm sorry, I see now. So, umm, are you married?" She asked. In my head, I'm like what's going on here? I was confused to be honest. Why would she want to talk to me? I mean not that I'm unattractive, but something about it wasn't sitting well with me. as impressed as I was with what I saw, I simply just looked down at my ring. She nodded he head and proceeded in the opposite direction. I did feel guilty as I watched her walking away. I was literally speechless during the conversation. I mean not one word, just gestures.

A couple days later, I got a phone call from my manager. I was suspended for harassment. A customer filed a complaint, claiming I groped them while reaching on a shelf. I was also accused of using vulgar language and being unprofessional. So much for being anonymous, I knew exactly who made the complaint. As I recall it, I was very professional. I mean I didn't utter a word. I was later given a date to come back and discuss the matter.

During the discussion, I explained my side of the story. I also insisted that they take a look back at the cameras if they hadn't already. They agreed. As the video showed, I made no physical contact, nor did I say anything in those moments. My manager asked," I thought you said you said nothing to her?" Unfortunately, the cameras had no audio. "I didn't." I replied.

"Well, in this frame, I clearly see you talking to the customer." He said. He was referring to me being in response to her needing help retrieving an item. I explained that to him, but he simply just shook his head.

"You're suspended for 5 days no pay." He said. The young lady was also banned from the store. I couldn't believe it. I've always seen forms of racial injustice, but it never happened to me personally. They believed her story with no hesitation and was ready to get rid of me over nothing. I figured they'd at least consider my character, but hey I guess not in these situations.

When I got home, I decided to tell my wife about the situation and of course she got upset. I'm certain apart of her thought I had done something considering the past. I couldn't blame her though.

After a while I began paying more attention to racial matters. This began to change my perception on life and the people around me. I felt myself becoming more political. I became more opinionated at work and around my peers. Some people liked the things I was passionate about, others stepped away. I was looked at differently at work so at that point I just didn't care anymore. My mind was no longer focused on working in the store. I was more focused in making a positive change in our communities.

Myself, my best friend, and his brother started a nonprofit organization called M.O.B., short for Minding Our Businesses. Its goal was to teach business, promote black businesses, and other community related services. Our organization grew rapidly. The name M.O.B. grew popularity quickly. I mean what can I say, it's a catchy acronym. On top of that, our great work never went unnoticed.

I began speaking on matters publicly. Racial and things that we do ourselves to disrupt the peace in our communities. With notoriety, there were definitely pros and cons. Being a black activist puts a target on your back for those who oppose you. Pros were the positive impact on so many lives. After a while, my mother began to voice her concerns. Saying things like be careful son. I mean she'd always tell me how proud she was so there wasn't any doubt about that. She made a statement that resonated with me. She said, "I'm proud of you but be careful out there. Nothing is worth your children growing up without a father." After that I slowed down on public activism and focused more on family and friends.

I finally found it in myself to quit my job. I was now being paid to do public speaking. This was such a great thing to me. Speaking the truth to my people and being paid to do so. What more could I ask for? I know my mother may think

I'm hardheaded, but this is what I wanted to do.

My speeches began to draw larger crowds. People wanted to hear what I had to say. I decided that now was the time to change my name to keep family and loved ones protected. I decided to call myself Rahim Farran. All my events were heavily secured. The manpower, in my opinion, created a sense of complacency. At my next speech, a large fight broke out. My best friend left the stage to help with crowd control. I see him grab an angry Caucasian guy from the brawl and then I heard gunshots. Right before my eyes he dropped. I rushed into the crowd towards him. The shooter was apprehended immediately. My best friend died that day. In a way

I felt like it was my fault. He died simply because someone didn't agree with the words I was speaking. We later found out the shooter was an off-duty police officer. His charges were dropped due to self-defense, probable cause, stand your ground, or some shit like that. All I know was it was a load of bull. The system has once again failed not only me, but the black community. This time it had hit home once more. My wife and I talked about it and we decided I should take a step back again because things were getting too dangerous. And they simply keep getting away with things they do. I went dark in my activism. No more speeches or events. Here I am jobless and falling apart mentally.

All I could think about was not letting my friend's death go in vein. Riots and protests were everywhere in regard to his wrongful execution. I sat quietly and didn't engage in any of it.

I got a knock at my door. It was his brother Jeremy. Cofounder of M.O.B. "What do you plan on doing brother?" He asked

"What can I do man?" I replied.

"Use your voice! Give the people hope. My brother didn't die so you can just shut up!" He said fiercely.

"But man, if I get killed then what?" I asked.

"Don't make excuses, this is your destiny. Make something happen!" He replied.

I began to think about it, "what if I had a more organized approach." I mean we were organized already so what now? I came up with a great idea. We were going to go black. Well anonymous in other terms. I decided I was going to create a secret society called The Black Circle. T.B.C. for short. I didn't know exactly how we would do it, but we needed a hidden approach to getting my message out to the people.

This group was meant to be as secretive as possible. We started off renting spaces on the basement floors of hospitals to host meetings. During the meetings I spoke anonymously via video with no visuals to the followers. There was also a voiceover to further protect my identity. One day I decided to attend one of the meetings. I was curious of the reactions to my teachings. So, I ended up prerecording the speech for that night. I noticed that there were a lot of people in attendance and the responses were impressive. Entering this meeting, I could feel the energy in the room. Once again, my words were impacting people on a grand scale. Dates and times for these meetings were encrypted and sent out in code to protect followers. Pat downs were also necessary for entering. I then decided that night that we needed a bigger place and one we could call our own.

We anonymously purchased an abandoned drug store in a predominantly black neighborhood. This definitely offered more privacy. We decided not to change the building's outer appearance. However, we completely overhauled the inside. We put up cameras, metal detectors, and built the seating in a circular fashion. The inside was painted black in its entirety. We built a circular platform right in the middle of the seating. Sitting atop the platform was a tinted booth with absolutely no transparency. The booth was created with bulletproof glass surrounding a podium. Inside the mic was sound technology to keep the speakers voice hidden. Underneath the platform was an escape route and/or pathway for me to use in case of emergency. We had this planned to the T. my idea was to attend the meetings like everyone else then maneuver my way out, into the pathway, then into the booth.

To make money we began to charge for attendance. This quickly became lucrative. Most of the money went back into the community through my nonprofit organization. Hope you didn't forget about M.O.B.! We now had more than enough funding. I was able to pay myself and my staff as well. The first couple meetings, there were no real speeches given. We just simply gave out instructions on how we'd take back our neighborhoods. These sessions weren't as responsive as the ones we had during the hospital basement days.

The next one we had, I decided to give a speech about revolution. This speech really got the crowd going. Not to mention we had a packed house that night. The instructions presented in the speech were not all legal per say but things needed to be done. For example, if foreigners wanted to keep their stores in our neighborhoods, they'd have to give up 10% of earnings to the organization for the betterment of our people or we'd physically shut it down. This was definitely extortion, but I didn't care. I want us to get ours. I also came up with some "no nonsense" policies. You may ask what that might entail. Well ANYONE who disrupts the peace in our communities would be dealt with at our discretion. We were taking it upon ourselves to enforce the law. We didn't care about race or gender, we just wanted to ensure peace. We felt like the police had failed us so many times before, so this was necessary.

The next meeting, we had, I noticed my mom showed up. This was a surprise for sure. Shortly afterwards she called me. "Son, I don't think this is a good idea. You're going to get yourself killed." She said with concern.

"Mom, no one knows who's giving the speeches or who runs the organization. Trust me okay. I love you." I replied.

I get home and reflect on things discussed at the meeting. I look over at my kids and begin to wonder if I'm in over my head. I know they need their father. My wife came over to me and said," you'll be ok babe. Remember why you're doing this and trust in your vision."

"Thank you, I needed to hear that." I replied while hugging them.

The next day we had a short meeting about how we'd approach the store owners. I decided we should take a week or two before actually trying the plan out. Then one of my members asked, "why wait? Let's try it now!" I was actually nervous that was why. I didn't say that, but I had never committed a crime so I'm certain my nerves would be on edge. So, I went with the flow and agreed.

"Let's do this then guys!" I said confidently. I asked myself on our way to the store, "what the fuck am I doing?"

We approached what was our 1st store to use. It was a pretty popular spot in this neighborhood. My first approach was to figure out if they were doing anything illegal and use that as leverage. I walked in and grabbed a bag of chips and a drink. I seen someone at the counter buying cigarettes by the single. In my head I'm like, "got your ass!"

"How you are doing today?" I asked the store owner/clerk.

"Good, sir, will this be all today." He replied as he rang me up.

"No, let me get 3 singles as well please." I replied.

"Okay, they're fifty cent a piece. Is that okay?" He asked.

"Actually, it isn't. Selling unpackaged cigarettes is illegal sir. I mean I'm not the police, but I can definitely get you in trouble." I said with confidence. He stood there in silence just staring at me. I knew then I had the advantage.

"This is how its going to go; every two weeks my accountant is to receive a detailed copy of your books and at the beginning of the month you're to pay my organization 10% of your earnings." I said calmly.

He laughed and said, "Get out my store before I call the police!"

I laughed knowing how bad the response time is in these types of neighborhoods. We decided to post up outside the store. As customers walked up, we simply told then the store was closed. This was easy at first, then people began wanting to check for themselves. The next few people walked in saying "damn store not closed." This went on until a couple of my members exposed their guns. That left people without question to go to another store. We did this for a little over an hour. I decided to approach the store owner before we left the store. "Business slowed down huh?" I asked sarcastically. He looked at me confused. This mf knows English! "Look we shut you down for about an hour just now with no problem and can continue to do so if you don't agree to our terms." I said. He began to reach for the phone. "Don't make that mistake sir, we can be violent if necessary. Put the phone down and agree!" I said with aggression. I gave him a burner cell with two numbers in it and left him with some instructions.

This was a successful takeover. In my gut, it felt so wrong, but this was for our people and we needed it. Over the next few weeks we continued to flex our muscle as we took over many other stores in the same manner. We even bought some out for fairly decent prices. We were now beginning to take back our neighborhoods. My nonprofit organization was also making some real noise and putting my hometown on the map. We were now an up and coming town once more. It seemed as if our town did a complete 360. Now it was time to discuss how we'd handle the crimes in our communities. Crime wasn't really a big issue by now. With that being said, there was still nonsense going on that I didn't like. My idea was to rough people up a bit for committing senseless crimes. That was a bit aggressive but we're here now so no turning back now. First situation we approached was an armed carjacking. We quickly tracked down the suspects and picked them up in our black van. My guys handled them, then dropped them off. We also returned the vehicle to its owner. I kind of felt bad for the suspects but hey it could have been worse if they were caught by police, right?

These were trying times for me believe it or not. Mentally I wasn't where I wanted to be. I allowed my demons to make me slip up and step out on my wife again. Thing is I wasn't feeling anything at that point and just continued.

Watching the news, I seen where another black male was killed due to police brutality. Another one of us failed by the system. And just like the others, no indictment. We decided to have a meeting at the drug store that night. We vowed to do something about these types of situations. Two targets were designated that night. The police officer from the news and the one who killed my best friend. We used social media to gather information on both the targets. We even created an expose group to expose racist and white supremacist. It was so surprising how many of people that were just beneath our noses. Our target list grew longer and longer. I'm now thinking, "what do we do to them?" Jeremy replied, "let us handle this. Keep your hands clean."

I had no idea how this would turn out, but I guess we were about to find out. My group voted in favor of paying them a visit and handling it physically. I wasn't too sure about this. I mean we were doing enough illegal shit as is. But on the contrary, we technically don't exist. We then loaded up and headed out to our first invasion. We chose to stake out the cop who killed Jeremy's brother home. Once it seemed like his home was settled, we made our move. We quickly took advantage and pulled him from his home. My heart was pounding. This was kidnapping! I then overheard a little voice say, "Daddy what's that noise?" I stopped right there and thought about my own children. "Farran! We are doing this!" Said Jeremy. I jumped back to reality as we rushed him to the van. He was taken to the basement of the drugstore shortly after. The other police officer was picked up that night as well. He too was dropped off at the drugstore and placed in the basement. Like clockwork, this was on the news! The van was caught on residential surveillance. No faces or bodies, just the van. We were sloppy. "We got to burn it." I said

"What about the targets?" Jeremy asked.

"That's up to y'all man. Just don't be sloppy." I replied.

"So, burn them in it?" Jeremy asked.

"I wouldn't advise it man. Just get the job done and I'll contact you all in two weeks." I said.

I thought by not specifically giving them instructions to commit murder, I wouldn't feel guilty. Well that wasn't true. Two weeks had passed, and I didn't even bother to ask about the targets from the basement. The list of targets became missing persons and were on the news. To me, this was a scary situation. I realized; we were doing this all wrong. I was then reminded of all the things that were done to us and that feeling of empathy faded with the quickness. We were determined to send a message. The news was calling us The Black Mob. Our totals were north of 25 people missing. What my group were doing with these people was outside of my knowledge. We were under investigation and there was a hefty reward for information regarding its members.

We decided to have our last meeting at the drugstore. During the meeting I took responsibility for the things that we were being accused of and basically said, there's more where that came from. We will not tolerate nonsense or racism. I had a hunch that someone in the crowd that night was with the FEDs. I made sure the message got across, so they'd know for themselves.

When I got home, I told my wife we had to move. She didn't even ask why. She began packing right then. We stopped by my mom's house on the way out of town. I told her I was moving. She said, "I understand son, be safe. I love y'all."

Thing is though, I still had some loose ends to tie up before I left town. The young lady I had an affair with knew about me and was upset and threatening to turn me in. I reached out to my group about it and without question they said they'd take care of it. The building was soon raided, and nothing was found but a burned van with human remains that matched the identities of two missing police officers. I had blood on my hands. I never intended for the organization to handle personal matters, but I panicked when I told them to handle the young lady. After some time, her being missing came back on me. I knew this would come eventually. I was brought in for questioning. I denied all allegations against me. For now, I was still "invisible". The investigation made its way to mainstream media. I was the prime suspect in the investigation. Members of the group and organization were questioned and accused as well. They were asked about who it was that's paying them or which one of them was the leader. During an interview, one of the investigators laughed when I was asked if I was the leader. I was clearly underestimated. This gave me a clear advantage in this case. No real arrests were made at this time, but we felt the pressure of the investigation. We all were followed, calls tapped, and I'm certain we were hacked as well. I couldn't believe it got to this point. What was intended to spread positivity and create equal opportunity quickly became evil. I was ready to attest for my sins at this point. I knew I was in too deep and decided I should just turn myself in. I began to separate myself from the world. I deleted my social media accounts, deleted emails, and destroyed my cell phone. I talked it all over with my wife and told her it would be best if she moved in with her parents for the time being. I needed to be alone in case things took a turn for the worse.

I called the police station anonymously from a burner cell to tip off my location. The cops showed up in no time along with other members of the law. I laid down on the floor as they surrounded my house. I closed my eyes the entire time. I was very much intimidated. I didn't know what was going to come of me at this point. When I opened my eyes, we were arriving at a holding center. I was later transferred to maximum security. I was told that my court date was in two weeks. I didn't care to call any of my family about me going to jail. I figured they had enough to worry about.

With the phone calls given to me, I called my legal team. These two weeks gave me some time to think about how thigs could play out. I knew truthfully, they had nothing on me. just my word saying I was responsible for it all. my lawyers and I came up with a game plan. I had reconvinced that the things I was doing with The Black Circle were justifiable and weren't nearly as bad as the things done to our people by secret societies from the opposing races. This attitude refueled my ambition to continue to impact our people. I mean plus, what real evidence would they have to connect me to any crime anyway. Crazy thing is the young lady that went missing was said to not be in connection with the crimes of the Mob. With that being said, now was the perfect time to test the system.

 My court date finally arrived. I was super nervous deep down. I thought to myself, either its time to get out and keep making a difference or go to jail for my crimes. I walked in the court room with my head held high. As they called out the charges, I was like damn! I chuckled a bit as we pleaded not guilty. The case that was presented on my behalf was that the "Mob" paid me to say I was the leader. I was nothing more than an ex manager of a grocery store that needed funding for his organization. The deal was to fully fund our projects if I agreed to take the fall for the crimes committed by the group. We also requested witness protection for leaking information. I described the building in which had already been raided and explained how come we couldn't see who the leader was. With the lack of evidence, they had no choice but to believe my story. The trial lasted 3 days and I was acquitted on all accounts. I was finally released and my request for witness protection was denied, which to me was strange. The home I was staying in was far from everyone anyways. All I needed were weapons.

The Black Circle was still in operation and I was still the leader. It was the opposing races that I wanted to stay hidden from. I continued to send assignments to my nonprofit organization M.O.B. to keep up the great work in the neighborhood. Though we lost a lot of funding due to the investigation, we were still able to provide services to those who needed us. My name had been circulating negatively as a snitch. Little do they know; I'm technically snitching on myself. This pushed them further away from figuring out who the leader of this group. The group and I kept in constant contact through more burner cell phone. We were still serving justice as Jeremy always says.

The Black Circle continued to headline the news but known to society as The Black Mob. Aggressive approaches continued as well throughout the group. Members were either branded with a circle or tattooed. More allegations rained down on my group. A few of the newer members were being brought in for questioning. They were fairly new, so they had no clue who the leader was. Well, they aren't supposed to. I was so far out of reach; I was unfamiliar of how things were being ran in my absence. I had been hearing about multiple members making deals with the FEDs. Members were killing other members based on allegations of being a leak. Honestly, I didn't know how I'd handle those types of situations so who am I to say anything.

I had really been missing my family lately. I felt now was a good time to move them back out to the home. I just wanted to live a normal life again, whatever that may be. I now had them back and I was grateful. My burner rang twice before I went to bed. I ignored the calls and didn't even bother to see who it was.

That morning we woke up and I noticed more missed calls. My wife and kids were getting ready to leave. She had to go to work and drop the kids off with their grandparents.

"Alright we'll see you later babe." My wife said.

"Okay see y'all later. Love you." I replied.

I called my mom shortly after.

(Phone ringing) "Hey mom! How you are doing?" I said.

"I'm great son. Where are you?" She replied.

"Ma, I can't tell you that. As a matter of fact, I can't talk now." I replied.

"But I miss…"

I hung up the phone before she could finish her sentence. I often think about the toll this life has taken on the people who are close to me. as I sit here daydreaming, I think about how life used to be. So simple, but I feel like this was my calling. Now I wonder how far this journey will take me.

"Open the door now! We know you're in here!"

Though I sit here in a daze, I hear this loud screaming from outside my door. I guess this could be the end of the journey perhaps.

Boom! Down comes my front door as police enter my home. I'm already on the floor with my hands behind my head. I knew, if given a reason, the police would have definitely taken me out. Especially considering the things I've been accused of.

Mr. Farran, you're under arrest!

I chuckled as they said my name. I go by Raheem Farran, it's just an alias. I felt the need to not go by my government name after a while. My previous charges included racketeering, conspiracy, murder, capital murder, kidnapping, domestic terrorism, etc. Charges that I beat. So, what the hell am I under arrest for?

"You know you one dumb nigger." Said one of the officers.

"Excuse me, watch your fucking tone and please refrain from speaking with me until we reach the station." I replied fiercely.

I see them look at each other and laugh. I overheard one of them say, "station?" as I sat there, I began to get a bit nervous. I haven't felt fearful in so long. The longer we ride, the more I think back on things wondering was it all worth it. Was I wrong? I feel the car gradually slowing down as we approach literally nothing. I began to do the math, white police, black man/criminal. I may just die here...

"Alright, get out boy!" The officers said to me.

"No sir." I replied calmly

They proceeded to drag me from the vehicle. All I see around me is wooded area and two police. I close my eyes as I began to talk to The Creator. Before I could get my words out a gunshot rang out. Pow! I was shot. I looked down and noticed a hole in my side the size of a bowl. I collapsed immediately. There I lay bleeding as the police sped off. Was this it for me? I close my eyes as fatigue begins to set in. Now, nothing, just darkness...

A voice came to me and said, "This is not it for you." I figured I'd die here, then my eyes began to reopen. I had lost so much blood. I began wondering about how those police even found my house or if they were even real officers. They didn't even bother to do a pat down. Which meant I still had my items in my pocket. I struggled but was able to get my cell from my pocket. I called Jeremy and sent him my location then destroyed the phone. He called my wife and told her what had happened. I had no idea if I'd even survive this.

I woke up in a hospital after being comatose for 3 days. I heard the officers responsible were found dead 2 days later. I knew right then it was The Black Circle once more. Arrests were made from the investigation in the so-called Black Mob case. Little did we know, most of the people we had targeted were apart of a secret group as well. One that expressed hate for people of color. We won that war. They were soon busted on many charges. I was questioned again but nothing linked me to any crimes. To this day The Black Circle is still in operation. Its still a secret organization but we do use less aggression in our approach. But please beware, we don't mind taking there.

Where destruction is the motive,
unity is dangerous.

-Ravi Zacharias

THE END